THE WoLF IS NoT INVITED

Avril McDonald

Illustrated by Tatiana Minina

Crown House Publishing Limited
www.crownhouse.co.uk

First published by

Crown House Publishing Ltd
Crown Buildings, Bancyfelin, Carmarthen, Wales, SA33 5ND, UK
www.crownhouse.co.uk

and

Crown House Publishing Company LLC
6 Trowbridge Drive, Suite 5, Bethel, CT 06801, USA
www.crownhousepublishing.com
© Avril McDonald, 2016

Illustrations by Tatiana Minina

British Library Cataloguing-in-Publication Data
A catalogue entry for this book is available from the British Library.

Print ISBN: 978-178583017-4
Mobi ISBN: 978-178583070-9
ePub ISBN: 978-178583071-6
ePDF ISBN: 978-178583072-3

LCCN 2015953329

Printed and bound in the UK by
Gomer Press, Llandysul, Ceredigion

For the wonderful love of true friendship.

Thanks to Åsa Pettersson for her inspiration and contribution to
Feel Brave's work and to the poet Robert Saxton for his editorial directive.

Deep in the forest,
a wolf and a cat
Played in a tree house.
Well, how about that!

Meet Wolfgang the brave
and a cat called Catreen,

Who might be the best friends
that you've ever seen.

They'd make up great stories of magical things
And dance by the moon using feathers for wings,

Laughing and singing and jumping about,
Having such fun all the stars would come out.

But one day they happened
to hear a strange sound.
A knock and a bark
made them both turn around.

They never expected
a knock at the door.
Well, no one had knocked
at their tree house before.

Wolfgang
+
Catreen
=
Best
Friends

"Who's there?" asked Catreen,
wondering who it might be.
"It's Clarissa," they heard.
"Will you come play with me?"

Clarissa was beautiful,
daring and fun,
Bright eyes like the moon
and gold hair like the sun.

Catreen started dreaming
of what they might do

And Wolfgang was certain
they'd let him play too.

They quickly got dressed
in their favourite clothes.
Clarissa just loved
the pink dress Catreen chose.

Then she said to them both
as she flicked back her hair,
"The wolf's NOT invited,
I don't want him there."

Wolfgang stood still,
    and his chest felt all tight.
Catreen couldn't leave him,
    that wouldn't be right!

But she ran off to play
    and she didn't look back …
Wolfgang's heart broke
    with a mighty great crack.

Quietly he cried,
    thinking no one could see …
But someone was watching
    from high in the tree.

"Oh Wolfgang," said Spider,
   "you know what to do.
Don't let your heart break
   though Catreen has left you.

There are things that you love
   to just do on your own,
Go and make some new fun
   then you won't feel alone."

"You love building things,"
called a voice from the sky.
"And you love to sing loud,"
said some friends, swinging by.

"Yes, I do love those things,"
    Wolfgang thought with a smile.
He decided to play by himself
    for a while.

It surprised him to hear
someone else at the door …

A kind wolf in big shoes
that he'd not met before.

"My name's Karl," said the wolf.
"I like building things too.
I have feathers for dancing.
Can I play with you?"

Then they flew in a spaceship
to a faraway land.
But Catreen wasn't having
the fun that she'd planned.

Clarissa was frightful,
so nasty and mean.
I'll teach her a lesson,
thought clever Catreen.

So she tossed a cream pie
    and it sailed through the air,
Then it plopped on Clarissa
    and messed up her hair.

She ran back to the tree house,
  but only to find
Someone else playing there,
  a strange wolf of some kind.

She'd hurt Wolfgang's feelings,
  so he wasn't sure
If he wanted to be
  Catreen's friend any more.

So she sat on the doorstep
  and waited outside.
How sorry she looked
  as she sat there and cried.

She waited and waited.
It felt like for years!
But he let her back in
once she'd dried all her tears.

And though they allowed her
to join in their game,
With Karl playing too
it just wasn't the same.

But Karl couldn't stay long,
he was moving that day,

To a place called New York,
a long plane ride away.

Catreen made some toast
and a nice cup of tea.
She wanted to say she was sorry,
you see.

She told Wolfgang the story
about the cream pie,
He laughed so much
that he started to cry.

And up in the tree house
a wolf and a cat
Were best friends again.
Well, how about that!